Other Oxford Books
by Val Biro

Hungarian Folk-tales

The Magic Doctor

Jack and the Robbers
(*text by Jill Bennett*)

The Hobyahs

The Pied Piper of Hamelin

The Donkey that Sneezed

The Odd Job Man and the
Thousand Mile Boots
(*text by Jean Kenward*)

Jack and the Beanstalk

The Three Little Pigs

What's up the Coconut Tree?
(*text by A. H. Benjamin*)

The Three Billy-Goats Gruff

The Show-Off Mouse
(*text by A. H. Benjamin*)

Lazy Jack

Hansel and Gretel

To Louise,
my model for Goldilocks,
with love

OXFORD
UNIVERSITY PRESS

Great Clarendon Street, Oxford OX2 6DP

Oxford New York
Athens Auckland Bangkok Bogotá Buenos Aires
Calcutta Cape Town Chennai Dar es Salaam
Delhi Florence Hong Kong Istanbul
Karachi Kuala Lumpur Madrid Melbourne
Mexico City Mumbai Nairobi Paris São Paulo
Singapore Taipei Tokyo Toronto Warsaw

with associated companies in
Berlin Ibadan

Oxford is a registered trade mark of Oxford University Press

British Library Cataloguing in Publication
Data available

ISBN 0–19–272391-X

Printed in Hong Kong

GOLDILOCKS
AND THE
THREE BEARS

Retold and illustrated by
Val Biro

OXFORD
UNIVERSITY PRESS

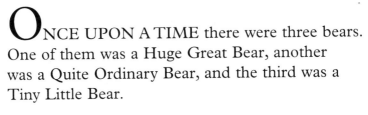

ONCE UPON A TIME there were three bears. One of them was a Huge Great Bear, another was a Quite Ordinary Bear, and the third was a Tiny Little Bear.

They lived in a cave in the middle of a great big wood.
But the inside of this cave was just like a house.

One day Quite Ordinary Bear cooked some porridge
and poured it into bowls: a huge bowl for Huge
Great Bear, an ordinary bowl for Quite Ordinary
Bear, and a little bowl for Tiny Little Bear.

But the porridge was too
hot, so the three bears
went out for a walk until
it cooled down.

Now, at the edge of the great big wood there lived a little girl called Goldilocks. Her mother kept telling her that she must never, *never* go into the great big wood on her own.

But on this day, when her mother wasn't looking, naughty little Goldilocks slipped out of the house and went into the great big wood all on her own! She was a *very* naughty little girl.

Goldilocks walked and skipped deeper and
deeper into the great big wood, and she saw
some squirrels, a badger, two owls, and a rabbit.
But she did not see any bears.

What she did see was the cave where the bears lived.
As there was no one around (and as Goldilocks was a
very naughty little girl), she went inside.

In the kitchen Goldilocks saw the porridge bowls, and she felt like having breakfast.

So she ate some of the porridge in the huge bowl, but it was too hot.

Then she tried the porridge in the ordinary bowl, but it was too cold.

But the porridge in the little bowl was just right, so naughty little Goldilocks ate it all up.

In the sitting room Goldilocks saw three chairs, and she felt like sitting down.

So she sat in the huge chair, but it was too hard.

Then she tried the ordinary chair, but it was too soft.

But the little chair was just right, except that as naughty little Goldilocks sat down, the chair broke into bits.

In the bedroom Goldilocks saw three beds, and she felt like having a nap.

So she lay down on the huge bed, but it was too hard.

Then she tried the ordinary bed, but it was too soft.

But the little bed was just right, so naughty little Goldilocks got in and was soon fast asleep.

Just then the three bears came home.

Huge Great Bear looked
at his bowl and said in a
big gruff voice:

'Somebody has been eating
my porridge!'

Quite Ordinary Bear looked
at her bowl and said in
an ordinary voice:

'And somebody has
been eating *my* porridge!'

Tiny Little Bear turned his
bowl upside down and cried
in a small piping voice:

'Somebody has eaten my porridge *all up*!'

Then Huge Great Bear looked at his chair
and said in a big gruff voice:

'Somebody has been sitting in my chair!'

Quite Ordinary Bear looked at her chair
and said in an ordinary voice:

'And somebody has been sitting
in *my* chair!'

Tiny Little Bear looked at
his broken chair and cried
in a small piping voice:

'Somebody has broken my chair
into bits!'

Then Huge Great Bear looked
at his bed and said in his biggest
and gruffest voice:

**'Somebody has been lying
in my bed!'**

Quite Ordinary Bear looked at her bed and said in her most ordinary voice:

'And somebody has been lying in *my* bed!'

But when Tiny Little Bear looked at his bed he cried out in his smallest, most piping voice:

'Somebody is lying in my bed *right now*!'

Goldilocks woke up and screamed when she saw three angry bears looking at her.

Goldilocks leapt out of bed
and ran out of the cave in a flash,

and the three bears chased her all
the way to the edge of the wood.

And there the bears stopped, because
they never left the great big wood.

But frightened little Goldilocks ran
on and on, until at last she was safely
in her mother's arms.